Handsome
and Gruesome

For Ruby Coplestone,
with Seriously Silly wishes
L.A.

For Tilly Mae, with love
A.R.

Visit Laurence Anholt's website at
www.anholt.co.uk

ORCHARD BOOKS
338 Euston Road
London NW1 3BH
Orchard Books Australia
Level 17/207 Kent Street, Sydney, NSW 2000

First published by Orchard Books in 2009

Text © Laurence Anholt 2009
Illustrations © Arthur Robins 2009

The rights of Laurence Anholt to be identified as the author
and of Arthur Robins to be identified as the illustrator
of this work have been asserted by them in accordance
with the Copyright, Designs and Patents Act, 1988.

A CIP catalogue record for this book is available from the British Library.

ISBN 978 1 84616 078 3 (hardback)
ISBN 978 1 84616 316 6 (paperback)

1 2 3 4 5 6 7 8 9 10 (hardback)
1 2 3 4 5 6 7 8 9 10 (paperback)

Printed in China

Orchard Books is a division of Hachette Children's Books,
an Hachette UK company.
www.hachette.co.uk

Laurence Anholt   Arthur Robins

seriously SILLY colour

Handsome and Gruesome

ORCHARD BOOKS

Once upon a toadstool sat two garden gnomes. Their names were Handsome and Gruesome. Handsome was a smart plastic gnome with a fishing rod.

But Gruesome was a tatty old gnome with peeling paint. She had been chewed by a puppy when she was little and she only had half a hat.

Handsome and Gruesome had lots of friends in the garden.
There were two rabbits, a wise Buddha, a hedgehog and a little stone boy who weed in the pond.

Everybody in the beautiful
garden would have been happy
if it hadn't been for the mean old
scarecrow. He looked after the
vegetable patch.
The scarecrow's job was
to frighten the little birds away,
but he liked to scare everybody
else as well.

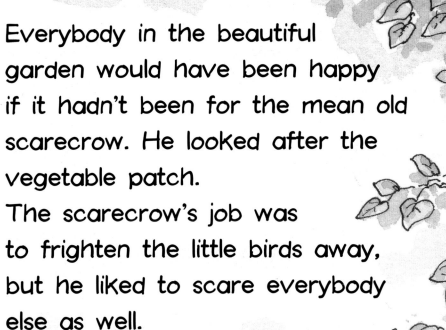

He told horrible stories about the gardener who owned the garden. "He is as big as a giant and has a dangerous lawnmower and an enormous dog. Snee hee hee!"

Everybody shivered with fear (except the Buddha, who was always calm).

The wicked scarecrow was
especially mean to poor Gruesome.
"This would be a pretty garden
if it wasn't for little Half Hat,"
he would say.

One spring day, Handsome and Gruesome met their friend the hedgehog. The two gnomes saw he had some litter stuck to his back.

Let us help you. Look, it has words on it.

Handsome and Gruesome could not read long words, so they went to find the wise Buddha.

"This is a Good Thing,"
said the Buddha.
"Who do you think will win?"
asked the rabbits, hopping
up and down.
"You know in your heart,"
said the Buddha.
"WEE WILL!" shouted
the little boy.
"Not when the gnome's at home,"
muttered the evil scarecrow.

That evening, as Handsome and Gruesome were curling up under the toadstool, they heard whispering from the vegetable patch. It was the scarecrow making an evil plan.

I will get rid of those gnomes for ever. Then we will win the garden competition. Snee hee hee!

Gruesome was terribly upset.
"Oh, Hammy, if it wasn't for my
ugly looks, that scarecrow would
leave you alone," she said.

As the moon came up, a long shadow fell across the toadstool. The scarecrow led the poor gnomes along the path, further than they had ever been before.

I'm taking you for a midnight picnic. Snee hee hee!

When they reached the wild part
of the garden, the horrible
scarecrow left them sitting in
a blackberry bush.
"Here's your picnic!" he said.
Then he went away laughing . . .
"Snee hee hee!"

A little tear rolled down
Gruesome's plastic cheek.

"Don't cry, Gruey," said Handsome,
pulling a thorn from his bottom.
"Look! I filled my fishing bag with
our little glow-worm friends and
I sprinkled them all along the
path behind us."

It was true! All they had to do
was follow the shiny path back
to the toadstool.
"Drat!" growled the scarecrow.
"Those nasty gnomes are home."

Very early the next morning, when the dew was still on the garden, the horrible scarecrow woke Handsome and Gruesome again. This time he took them to the very bottom of the garden . . .

"Snee yer later, mashed potater!"

"Oh, Hammy! This time we are really lost," wailed Gruesome.

"Don't worry, Gruey, I have another plan. I filled my fishing bag with little snails and scattered them all along the path."
"Oh, Hammy, you are so clever," said Gruesome, clapping her hands.

But Handsome was not so clever.
All the little robins flew out of the
trees and ate the little snails.

This time Handsome and
Gruesome were really lost.
All day they stumbled through
long nettles and broken
flower pots.

As it began to get dark, they came to a clearing. And there stood a funny little house with a light at the window.

Handsome and Gruesome were so tired, they curled up on the doorstep.

Suddenly a huge hand reached out and pulled the little gnomes inside.

It was the Gardener!

Handsome waited outside. He
wondered if he would ever see
Gruesome again.

At last the door opened.
Out came a gnome. She was
very beautiful with a lovely
painted face and a flower
on her tall hat.

The Gardener pushed them back
along the path to the toadstool.

"There now," said the Gardener.
"Everything is ready for the
competition. The vegetables are
fat. My flowers have never been
better. But the prettiest things in
the garden are my lovely gnomes.

All I need to do is get rid of
this old scarecrow."
But just as the Gardener was
about to carry the scarecrow
to the bonfire, the garden gate
swung open and in walked two
ladies. They were the judges from
the Best Garden Competition.

"Congratulations!" they said.
"You have won First Prize!"

A man from the newspaper came
too. "What lovely gnomes!" he said.

Everyone had their photo taken.
They were very proud of their
beautiful garden.

Everyone except the mean old scarecrow, lying on the compost heap at the bottom of the garden.

Enjoy all these Seriously Silly stories!

All priced at £8.99

Orchard books are available from all good bookshops, or can be ordered direct from the publisher:
Orchard Books, PO BOX 29, Douglas IM99 1BQ
Credit card orders please telephone: 01624 836000 or fax: 01624 837033
or visit our website: www.orchardbooks.co.uk or e-mail: bookshop@enterprise.net for details.

To order please quote title, author and ISBN and your full name and address.
Cheques and postal orders should be made payable to 'Bookpost plc.'
Postage and packing is FREE within the UK (overseas customers should add £1.00 per book).

Prices and availability are subject to change.